Early Prevention Series

THE KOALA WHO WOULDN'T COOPERATE

A Story About Responsible Behavior

by Lawrence E. Shapiro, Ph.D.
illustrated by Steve Harpster

THE KOALA WHO WOULDN'T COOPERATE

A Story About Responsible Behavior

by Lawrence E. Shapiro, Ph.D.
illustrated by Steve Harpster

Childswork/Childsplay publishes products for mental health professionals, teachers, and parents who wish to help children with their developmental, social, and emotional growth. For questions and comments, call 1-800-962-1141.

A Brand of The Guidance Group
www.guidance-group.com

Printed in the United States of America

ISBN 10: 1-58815-066-6
ISBN 13: 978-1-58815-066-0

Introduction

Many parents and teachers complain about children who are uncooperative. They naturally want children to follow rules, be considerate, and do what they are asked to with a positive attitude, yet many children find these simple behaviors hard.

There are many reasons why we are seeing so many more uncooperative, difficult, and even oppositional children, but most experts agree that this kind of behavior comes from lowered expectations, a permissive attitude in the home, and poor role models.

Being uncooperative is not just annoying to others; it often portends more serious behavior problems as well. It reflects an unwillingness to respect adult authority and an inability to see the consequences of one's behavior. When young children get into a pattern of being uncooperative and willful, they become predisposed towards more serious misbehavior as they grow older.

In this story, Charlie has a hard time learning to be more responsible and respectful to adults. When he was younger, he could pretty much do anything he liked, but as he gets older, he is expected to be more cooperative and do what adults ask of him. Like many children, he hasn't learned from the negative reactions to his uncooperative behavior. Fortunately, his older brother has a more easygoing temperament and teaches Charlie that he can make better choices about his behavior, and that doing so will help him get the positive attention from adults that all children need.

The Childswork/Childsplay Early Prevention Series is designed to help young children learn about common emotional and behavioral problems and acquire skills that can help prevent these problems from becoming serious. To make a significant difference in a child's emotional and behavioral development, you should take a few minutes a day to teach and reinforce cooperativeness, kindness, and compassion. It is never too early or too late to teach the importance of being cooperative.

-Lawrence E. Shapiro, Ph.D.

Activity Sheet

The Charlie doll that comes with this book can be used to help reinforce the lessons of *The Koala Who Wouldn't Cooperate*. You can use the doll with the following play activities to teach and reinforce new behavioral skills.

Role Play

The adult can narrate the story and the child, using the doll, can take the role of Charlie. After the story, take time to ask the child questions, such as:

"Do you think you are like Charlie?"
"Do you sometimes have trouble cooperating or following the rules?"
"Who do you know that is always cooperative?"

Make Up a Story or Play

You can also encourage children to make up their own story or play, using Charlie with other dolls or stuffed animals. For example, you might use other stuffed bears to represent Charlie's family members and enact plays where Charlie shows how good his behavior has become.

You may also want to make a videotape of the dolls acting out a story, which the child can then watch. Viewing positive scenes can help the child internalize the messages of the book.

Use the Doll as a Reminder of the Importance of Behaving Responsibly

Young children often attribute magical powers to their toys. A child may want to have the Charlie doll as a playmate or bedtime companion. Just having the doll can serve as a reminder that responsible behavior will help them build rewarding relationships.

When Charlie was a little koala, everyone thought he was cute. He would stand on his head and make funny faces. He would stick out his tongue with food on it. He would whirl around in circles until he fell over.

Even when Charlie's antics caused a problem, his parents didn't seem to mind.

Once, when Charlie was balancing himself on top of his chair, he spilled his juice all over the rug, and he started to cry. But his mother said, "That's okay, Charlie. Everyone makes mistakes," and she tickled him until he laughed.

Charlie felt like anything he did was cute. Anything he did would be okay.

But as Charlie got older, the things he did when he was young didn't seem so cute to his parents.

Once his mother said, "It's time for dinner, Charlie." But instead of coming to dinner, Charlie stood on his head and stuck out his tongue.

"Charlie, stop that!" his mother said, but Charlie thought it was funny so he didn't stop. Then his mother got mad at Charlie for not listening.

Another time, Charlie's father said, "Charlie, it's time to get ready for bed."

But Charlie was having fun doing cartwheels around the living room, and so he kept on doing them.

His father got mad at Charlie for not listening. He crossed his arms on his chest and scowled. He said, "Charlie, you're not going to get any allowance this week."

And Charlie thought that his father was becoming very mean.

One day, his grandma said, "Charlie, let's help your mother and clean up the toys that are all over your room."

But Charlie wanted to keep on playing with his cars and trucks.

He said, "I don't want to clean up my toys now. I'll clean them up later."

His grandma just shook her head and said, "Charlie, why can't you just do what people ask you the first time? Why can't you just cooperate?"

But Charlie didn't have a good answer for this question. He just kept on doing whatever he liked.

Charlie's brother, Henry, was very different. Henry was five years older than Charlie, but it seemed like he had always been a more cooperative koala.

When his mother said, "Henry, it's time to eat dinner," Henry would stop what he was doing, wash his hands, and come straight to the dinner table. Sometimes he would even help his mother put the plates and silverware out on the table.

When his father said, "Henry, it's time to brush your teeth and get ready for bed," Henry would say, "Okay, Dad." He would go right upstairs to change into his pajamas and wash his face and brush his teeth. Henry knew just what to do to get ready for bed, and he liked to see his father smile at him when he did things just right.

When his grandma said, "Henry, can you clean up your toys?" Henry would do it right away. He liked to see how fast he could put his toys away.

As Charlie and Henry got even older, it seemed to Charlie that he got punished more and more often. It also seemed to him that Henry did anything he wanted to do and got everything he wanted.

Charlie lost his TV privileges. Henry got to stay up late and watch his favorite show.

Charlie got his allowance taken away for a month. Henry got his allowance raised to three dollars.

Charlie wasn't allowed to ride his bike without his parents around. Henry got permission to ride his bike with his friends.

Charlie didn't think things were very fair.

"Why are you nicer to Henry than you are to me?" Charlie asked his mom. "Do you love Henry more?"

"Of course not," Charlie's mother said. "What a silly thing to say." But it still seemed to Charlie that it was true.

Charlie felt like his parents loved Henry better than him and treated him better, too.

Charlie thought his parents were not fair at all.

Charlie also thought his teacher, Mr. Nottingham, wasn't fair.

Mr. Nottingham was always telling Charlie what to do.

When Charlie took out a top from his pocket and spun it on his desk, Mr. Nottingham said, "Put that down, Charlie!"

When Charlie drew mazes on his math worksheets, Mr. Nottingham said, "Just do your work and stop playing around, Charlie."

When Charlie ignored the fact that it was time for silent reading and started talking to Nate, Mr. Nottingham said, "Stop talking, Charlie, or you are going straight to the principal's office."

Charlie felt like nothing he did would ever be right, and he became more and more angry.

He was angry at his parents. He was angry at his teacher. He was even angry at his grandmother, although not really as much as at the other adults.

And the angrier Charlie got, the more he felt like he shouldn't do what his parents and teacher wanted him to. Charlie thought, "No matter what I do, they won't be fair to me."

But for some reason, Charlie wasn't angry at Henry.

Even though Henry got to stay up later than Charlie, and even though Henry got more allowance, and even though Henry got to ride his bike with his friends, Charlie still loved his older brother. He wanted to be like Henry.

One day, Henry sat down on the bed next to Charlie. It had not been a good day at all for Charlie. He had come home from school with a note from his teacher saying that he had talked back in class, and his parents had sent him to his room. Dad had said, "I want you to think about your behavior, Charlie."

"We need to have a talk," Henry said.

"You're always in trouble, and you're always angry," Henry began, "but things don't have to be that way. If you just learn to think about the way you act and the way that grown-ups treat you when you misbehave, you'll see that when you are more cooperative, you are happier."

Charlie had heard this advice before. His parents were always saying, "Think about what you are doing."

His teacher was always asking, "Why do you always act so difficult? If you were just more cooperative, you'd do really well at school."

But Charlie didn't know why he acted the way he did. He just did.

"The important things to remember," Henry went on, "is that you always have a choice. One choice will make people happy with your behavior, and another choice will make them mad. The right choice will get you smiles and hugs and sometimes even treats. The wrong choice will get you angry words and looks and punishment.

"For example, when Mom says it is time for dinner, you can choose to listen and cooperate. That's the right choice. Or you can chose to ignore Mom and continue to play with your toys, and that's the wrong choice. Why is that the wrong choice?"

"Because Mom and Dad will be mad at me," Charlie said.

"That's right!" Henry said. "The right choice will make you feel good, but the wrong choice will make you feel bad. It's like a game. When you make the right choices, you will be the winner, but if you make the wrong choices, you will be the loser."

"You know what?" Henry asked.

"What?" Charlie answered.

"I just got a great idea." Henry paused for a minute to think about his idea.

"Let's make up a game about right and wrong choices. I'm going to write down five choices on five cards and then mix them up in a shoebox."

Henry got a stack of blank cards and a pencil from his desk. Then he went to his closet to find a shoebox.

Here are the five cards Henry wrote:

1. Your teacher asks you to do your work.
2. The stoplight says "Don't Walk."
3. You see a dollar bill lying on the kitchen floor.
4. Dad says it is time to get ready for school.
5. Mom asks you to get ready for bed.

Your teacher asks you to do your work.
The stoplight says “Don't Walk.”
You see a dollar bill lying on the kitchen floor.
Dad says it is time to get ready for school.
Mom asks you to get ready for bed.

"Now, I want you to close your eyes and pick a card," said Henry.

Charlie put one paw over his eyes and reached into the shoebox with the other one. He picked out a card, and Henry read it.

The card said, "You see a dollar bill lying on the kitchen floor."

"What do you think you should do if you see a dollar bill lying on the floor? What is the right choice and what is the wrong choice?" Henry asked.

Charlie thought that was an easy question.

"The right choice is to ask your mom or dad if they lost some money and to give it to them. The wrong choice would be to keep it for yourself and not tell anyone. That would be like stealing."

"That's right," said Henry. "That's exactly right."

And then Henry said, "Now try another card."

Charlie reached into the box again and picked a second card. Henry read it out loud. It said, "Mom asks you to get ready for bed."

"What do you think about this card?" Henry asked his brother.

Again, Charlie knew the answer right away. "The right thing is to do what your mother asks and get ready for bed. The wrong thing would be to complain or just keep on playing."

"Very good!" Henry said. "You really do know how to make the right choices, don't you?"

"I like this game," Charlie said. "I'm good at it, aren't I?"

"Yes, you are," Henry said. "You are very good at knowing how to cooperate."

"What is this game called?" Charlie asked.

"Well," said Henry, "let's call it Charlie's Cooperative Game."

"Can we play it some more?" Charlie asked.

"Sure," Henry said. "I'll make more cards, and we can play it as much as you like."

Henry made up lots of cards for Charlie's Cooperative Game, and Charlie and Henry played the game every day.

Sometimes Charlie's parents and grandma would play, too. Everyone was impressed with how good Charlie was at making the right choices.

And the more Charlie played the game, the more he started to make the right choices in real life.

He came to the table when he was called for dinner. He did his homework at exactly the right time. He got ready for bed as soon as he was asked, without a word of complaint.

One night, when his dad was tucking Charlie in, he gave him an extra-big koala-bear hug.

"You've become such a cooperative koala," Charlie's dad said. "We're all very proud of you!"

Ready for sleep, Charlie closed his eyes with a big smile on his face.

"Sweet dreams," his father said.

"Thank you," Charlie said back. "Sweet dreams to you, too."